W9-BNO-534

Bernie

The Beagle Who Liked German Cooking

Bernie

The Beagle Who Liked German Cooking

by Jean Rossbach
Pictures by Cathy Bobak

Bradbury Press · New York

Maxwell Macmillan Canada · Toronto
Maxwell Macmillan International
New York · Oxford · Singapore · Sydney

Text copyright © 1991 by Jean Rossbach
Illustrations copyright © 1991 by Cathy Bobak

All rights reserved. No part of this book may be reproduced or
transmitted in any form or by any means, electronic or mechanical,
including photocopying, recording, or by any information storage and
retrieval system, without permission in writing from the Publisher.

Bradbury Press
Macmillan Publishing Company
866 Third Avenue
New York, NY 10022

Maxwell Macmillan Canada, Inc.
1200 Eglinton Avenue East
Suite 200
Don Mills, Ontario M3C 3N1

Macmillan Publishing Company is part
of the Maxwell Communication Group
of Companies.

First edition
Printed and bound in the United States of America
10   9   8   7   6   5   4   3   2   1

The text of this book is set in Aster.
The illustrations are rendered in black marker.
Book design by Julie Quan and Cathy Bobak

Library of Congress Cataloging-in-Publication Data
Rossbach, Jean.
Bernie, the beagle who liked German cooking / by Jean Rossbach.—
1st ed.
p.   cm.
Summary: The adventures of Bernie, a beagle whose talent for
German cooking helps him succeed in life.
ISBN 0-02-777787-1
[1. Dogs—Fiction.   2. Cookery—Fiction.]   I. Title.
PZ7.R71998Be   1991
[E]—dc20   90-21782

To Rachel,
Sara, and Adam

CONTENTS

Bernie

The Beagle Who Liked German Cooking

Chapter One

੭੭੭

Oxtail Soup and
Pigs' Knuckles

One warm spring morning when the pussy willows were beginning to pop out, Mr. Gruber went to the pet store to buy a puppy.

He studied them all carefully.

Some were playfully snapping at one another. Some were eating. Some were sleeping, nestled close to one another.

One puppy, a little brown-and-white beagle, looked at Mr. Gruber and wagged its tail hopefully. Mr. Gruber nodded. "I think you're the one I want,"

he said. "And I'm going to name you Bernie, because that was the name of an old friend of mine who once went hunting with me in Germany. And you and I are going to go hunting together."

Mr. Gruber bought Bernie a red collar and a small leash. "Red looks good on beagles," he said approvingly.

He wrapped Bernie in an old blanket, because it had begun to rain, and carried him out to the car.

When Mr. Gruber arrived home, he showed Bernie proudly to Mrs. Gruber. "What do you think of this, Berta?" he asked.

Mrs. Gruber looked at Bernie disapprovingly. "What kind of dog is that?" she asked.

"A beagle," replied Mr. Gruber.

"Hmpphhh! I would rather have had a German shepherd!"

"We're in this country now, Mama," said Mr. Gruber, "and beagles are popular here. Bernie's going to go hunting with me."

Soon, on a cloudy afternoon, Mr. Gruber loaded his hunting equipment into his pickup truck and put Bernie in the back. "Don't jump out, now!" Mr. Gruber warned.

Bernie hung on tightly as the truck bumped and rolled along. *Oh boy,* he thought, looking up into the sky apprehensively, *we're going to have rain and here I am in the back of a truck. I'll catch my death of a cold!*

Mr. Gruber really enjoyed hunting; Bernie soon found that he didn't. Most of the time, he just snuffled through the underbrush or simply stretched out in the warm sun till it was time to go home. Once in a while, he scared up a rabbit, but he made no attempt to chase it. *It simply doesn't make sense to me,* he said to himself.

One day he noticed Mr. Gruber looking at him sadly.

"You know, Bernie," said Mr. Gruber, "you're something of a disappointment. I don't think you really care for hunting. What *do* you like anyway?" And he scratched Bernie under the chin in a kindly manner. "I don't think you'd get along with Mama, lying around the house."

But that's just where Bernie soon found himself, because in a short time Mr. Gruber quit taking Bernie out with him.

"He'll just get lost with me," he told his wife.

"So let him get lost," she said roughly. "He's no good anyway."

Bernie tried to stay out of trouble. He spent most of his time in the wicker dog bed with the soft plaid cushion that Mr. Gruber had bought him. His water bowl and feeding dish were nearby. He had even been provided with a few chew toys to play with: a ball with a bell in it and a rawhide bone shaped like a pork chop.

Mrs. Gruber continued to be unfriendly.

"Don't think I'm going to buy dog food for that no-good dog," she said unkindly. "He'll eat table scraps or nothing at all."

As it happened, Mrs. Gruber was an excellent cook and Bernie had few complaints about his meals. One of his favorites was rabbit stew with tender little potato dumplings. *But a bit too much flour in the dough,* he said to himself one day, *and the rabbit was somewhat overcooked. I think I could do better than that.*

One morning Mrs. Gruber decided to make home-made noodles, and she left the dough to rise in a pan near the stove while she went shopping.

I think I'll roll out the dough and cut the noodles for her, Bernie decided. *She usually makes them too thick anyway.* And he did just that. He rolled out the dough carefully and then cut it in neat floury strips, which he left to dry on the kitchen table.

When Mrs. Gruber arrived home, she went to the kitchen and saw the noodles. "Nicely done," she said, lifting up a noodle or two, "but who . . . ?" She turned quickly to look at Bernie, who was safely back in his dog bed by then, and then shook her head. "Not likely!" she said.

From then on, when Mrs. Gruber was gone, Bernie
helped out secretly in the kitchen. He tasted and
seasoned whatever was cooking on the stove and got
to be quite expert at it. When he had time, he looked
through her cookbooks.

"That was the best sauerkraut and pigs' knuckles you've ever made, Mama," Mr. Gruber said to his wife one night at dinner. "I've always said a touch of caraway seed brings out the flavor of the kraut."

Mrs. Gruber frowned. *Caraway seed? I never use caraway seed in sauerkraut. I didn't even know I had any.* (Bernie had found the caraway seed pushed way to the back of Mrs. Gruber's spice cabinet.)

"And that apple tart!" said Mr. Gruber enthusiastically. "*Delicious* taste! Did you use brown sugar or molasses?"

Molasses, thought Bernie with satisfaction.

After a while, Mrs. Gruber began to be suspicious. *Something's going on in my kitchen,* she told herself, *and I'm going to find out what it is!*

Soon thereafter she pretended to go out shopping.

"I'm going to the grocery—eggs are on sale!" she called loudly to no one in particular. "I'll see you later!" And she slammed the front door as if she were leaving. Then she positioned herself to watch through the kitchen window. A large pot of oxtail soup was simmering on the stove.

After a few minutes, Mrs. Gruber saw Bernie leave his bed, go slowly over to the kitchen cabinet, climb up on a chair, and select a small can, which he took over to the stove. He lifted the pot lid—using a pot holder, of course—and sprinkled something into the stew. Mrs. Gruber rushed into the kitchen.

"So I've caught you, you no-good dog! What is that you've just put in the stew?" And she pushed Bernie angrily off the chair.

"A touch of cinnamon!" Bernie answered hurriedly, tail between his legs. "It brings out the flavor of the meat!"

Needless to say, the discovery of Bernie's cooking ended his days in the Gruber household, even though Mr. Gruber protested, "We've got an unusual dog here, Mama!"

"*Too* unusual," she answered grumpily. "I'll tell

you, nobody—especially not a dog—fools around in *my* kitchen!"

Bernie soon found himself out on the street. "I don't like this, Mama," Mr. Gruber had said. "He won't have anyplace to go, or anything to eat."

"That's his problem," said Mrs. Gruber coldly.

For a while, Bernie hung around the neighborhood, hoping to be taken back in by the Grubers, but Mrs. Gruber always chased him away with a broom. *She's really serious!* Bernie thought.

Finally he left. As he was going down the street, he turned around and yelled to Mrs. Gruber, "Phooey on you *and* your cooking! Your vegetables were always overdone and your rice was too dry!"

Mrs. Gruber grunted and pitched the broom after him. Bernie trotted off quickly down the street. He was on his own now.

Chapter Two

Hard Times

It was August and the weather was hot and dry. Bernie thought longingly of his old comfortable bed with feeding dish and water bowl nearby. Especially of the water bowl. *Oh boy, am I thirsty!* he thought.

At first he wasn't sure what to do. For a while, he just stood on the sidewalk, his tongue hanging out, and watched the cars go by. Once he had to jump back quickly when a small car came whizzing around the corner unexpectedly. *Whew, that was a close one!* he thought. *A dog could get killed around here!*

Soon, when hunger began to gnaw in his stomach, Bernie hunted food—in alleys and around garbage cans. *I've really fallen on hard times,* he said to himself.

One evening he was nosing through a trash bag. Watermelon rinds . . . tea bags . . . rotten tomatoes . . . a pork-chop bone. A pork-chop bone! Bernie grabbed the bone and carried it to a hiding place under an old pile of lumber, where he quickly pulled off all the meat that was left. There wasn't much, but he chewed on the bone for a long time. Competition for food was fierce on the streets.

Eventually, Bernie made two friends: one, an Irish setter named Red; the other, a poodle named Cutie.

"My coat was once clean and glossy," boasted Red. "I was brushed regularly. One year I even got a blue ribbon for Best-of-Show!"

"What happened?" asked Bernie, eyeing Red's bedraggled coat with dismay.

Red sighed. "My owner died and I was given to a new family, but they couldn't keep me."

"So you ended up . . ."

"Here," said Red glumly.

"What about you, Cutie?" asked Bernie. "You look even worse!"

"You wouldn't believe how nice I once looked," she said proudly. She lifted a foot. "I used to have little balls of fur around my ankles and at the end of my tail." They all looked around at her tail. "And by my left ear," she continued, "I had a tiny bow made of pink rhinestones."

The three friends stayed together, roaming back-yards and alleys. They were often in trouble.

"There are a lot of unfriendly people out here!" Bernie said indignantly one day after the three of them had been chased from the back of a grocery store.

"Did you get anything?" asked Red. "I just about had a bag of gummy bears!"

"They're good!" said Bernie. "You can chew on them a long time!"

"I like the lemon-flavored ones," said Cutie.

Sometimes the friends got lucky. One afternoon, through an alley fence, they spotted some children having a picnic. The children had a carton of milk and a plate of cookies. Bernie, Red, and Cutie were *very* hungry.

"Can you sit up?" Red asked Bernie quickly. "Children love it when a dog sits up and begs. They'll feed you. Maybe you can get something for us, too."

"I never have done that," said Bernie, "but I think I know what you mean. Is it like this?" And he bounced back on his haunches with his front paws in the air. He had to practice it a few times to keep his balance.

Red looked at Bernie with a critical eye. "Keep your back straight and look friendly. I think you'll do!"

Bernie edged through an opening in the gate. When the children spotted him, they ran toward him.

For the next hour or so, while his friends waited patiently in the alley, Bernie played with the children. He sat up many times and tried to figure out what the children wanted him to say when they said, "Speak! Speak!" to him. He got lots of popcorn and a little doll plate of milk. He also got a ride in a baby carriage.

Finally, when he noticed the children were losing interest in him and playing with other things, he made his move.

He had seen a full box of animal crackers on the picnic table. Animal crackers would do nicely for an afternoon meal for Red and Cutie. When the children weren't looking, he grabbed the box by its little string and ran through the gate out into the alley.

"Quick, follow me!" he called to his friends. "I've got something!" The three of them ran as fast as they could down the alley till they reached a safe spot in a park. There they ate the animal crackers.

"The elephants are the best ones," said Red. "They're the biggest."

August edged into September. A few yellow and brown leaves were beginning to drift across the streets. The days had an end-of-season feel about them. Late one Sunday afternoon, Bernie came to a decision.

"There's no future for me around here," he told his friends. "Life like this is too hard. I'm going to try to find a job."

"Doing what?" Red asked, his forehead wrinkling.

"I'd like to work in a restaurant," Bernie answered.

"A restaurant?" questioned Cutie.

"Yes," said Bernie. "I've been thinking about it, and I'm going to head downtown to the employment office."

"Do you know where it is?" asked Red. "I don't think they'll let you in."

"Well, I'm going to try," said Bernie. "With a little luck, I'll find something."

Red shook his head doubtfully.

Soon, reluctantly, Bernie parted from his friends.

"Do you have to go?" asked Cutie. "We were having fun."

"I may see you again," Bernie said, "when times are better. Be careful, and watch out for those small cars. They move up on you fast!"

For a moment, Bernie looked affectionately at his friends, then watched them turn and go up the street. Night was coming and big raindrops were beginning to fall. Bernie saw Red duck away from a man who pointed an umbrella at him.

"Good-bye!" Bernie called. "I hope you find some-place dry to sleep!" But his friends were already out of sight by that time. He turned and headed toward the glow on the horizon that he knew meant down-town.

Chapter Three

Persistence Pays Off

Early Monday morning, Bernie made his way to the employment office. The day was dark and rain was falling. A few people with umbrellas up were gathered in front of the building waiting for the doors to open.

Bernie huddled in an alley close by. Suddenly a big gray cat came around the corner, saw Bernie, and stopped. Quickly it arched its back, fur raised, in warning.

Bernie looked at the cat and shook

his head. "Don't worry. I'm not going to chase you."

Gradually, the cat relaxed, but it didn't take its round yellow eyes off Bernie. "You aren't?" it asked.

"No," Bernie answered. "I'm here for something else."

The cat looked at Bernie. "You are? For what? For somebody to adopt you? I've tried that, too, but I haven't had any luck."

"No," said Bernie. "I'm waiting to apply for a job."

The cat stared at Bernie for a moment or two. "A job?"

"Yes," said Bernie. "I want to work in a restaurant."

"Oh," said the cat, nodding. "I understand. For food. Yes. Good idea. But what can you do?"

"I can cook," answered Bernie. "My specialty is German cooking."

The cat frowned.

"Have you ever heard of apple strudel?" Bernie asked. "Black Forest torte? Wiener schnitzel?"

The cat shook its head slowly. "I used to like tuna fish. . . ."

"Tuna fish, hmm. I really don't know of any German recipes using tuna fish, but I'm sure there are some."

"I just like it plain," said the cat hopefully, then added, "but I doubt if I'll ever get any again."

"Of course you will!" said Bernie encouragingly.

"Have you ever heard of catnip?" the cat asked.

"Catnip?"

"Yes. Can you cook anything using catnip? I'd love to eat that," the cat said.

"No-o-o-o," Bernie answered slowly. "What is it? An herb? A spice?"

"An herb, I think," said the cat, and it added wistfully, "I had some in a ball once. A blue catnip ball."

Bernie looked the cat over. He could see it had been in some fights. One of its ears was torn. "Have you ever had a home?" he asked.

"I think I did . . . a long time ago," the cat answered. "I remember a saucer of warm milk—and the tuna fish, of course—and a soft rug."

"I remember things like that, too," said Bernie. "A warm bed . . . a water bowl. My ball and pork-chop bone."

"A ball?" asked the cat. "Was it made of yarn?"

The employment office was opening and people were filing in.

"Well," said Bernie, "they're open for business. I must be going." He got to his feet, giving the cat a scare. To reassure it, he said, "Good luck! And keep up your spirits!"

The cat followed Bernie to the door of the employment office, and then sat down on a step. The rain had stopped and the sun was coming out.

"Look for a rainbow!" Bernie said cheerfully to the

cat, who was already beginning to feel sleepy in the sun. "And if I locate any catnip, I'll look you up!" Then he followed a woman through the door and into the employment office.

"I'm here to see an employment counselor," said Bernie, "about a job."

The clerk looked at Bernie for a moment, then gestured toward the door. "Go on! Get out of here! Shoo!"

"Now wait just a minute," protested Bernie. "I have a right to . . . " But the clerk had grabbed a newspaper and was already starting around the counter. Bernie tucked his tail between his legs and headed quickly for the door. "Grouch!" he said.

(Bernie only *pretended* to be leaving. In fact, when the clerk wasn't looking, he got right back into another line. Beagles can be very persistent.)

No one paid any attention to him. He moved along in place till he reached the counter again. The clerk—a different one—didn't see him at first. The man behind Bernie smiled and gestured down. "This fellow's next," he said.

The clerk looked over the counter and saw Bernie. "And what do you want to apply for, old boy?" he asked kindly. "Want to chase cars? Fetch newspapers?"

"No," answered Bernie solemnly, "as a matter of fact, I want to work in a restaurant. A German one, preferably."

"And what are your qualifications?" asked the clerk, smiling.

"I was a member of the Gruber household," answered Bernie. "They were formerly of Germany—Stuttgart, I believe—and while I was there, I learned the art of German cooking. I doubt if there's anybody in town who can roll out a better apple strudel than I can. I—"

"Ahem," interrupted the clerk. "I'm sorry. I don't believe we can help you. Maybe we could locate a restaurant where there's a cat problem, or a junkyard that needs a dog for protection. Although"—the clerk looked down at Bernie—"you're really rather small for that."

"I see," said Bernie, somewhat deflated. He thought for a moment. "Well, then, could you direct me to a telephone? I'd like to make a call."

The clerk smiled and pointed to a corner of the office. "Right over there," he said.

"Thank you," said Bernie.

"Good luck," said the clerk, and he turned to the next person in line.

Bernie walked purposefully over to the telephone. There, he jumped up onto a chair and, with his paws, opened a directory that lay on a small table. He leafed quickly through the yellow pages till he came to "Restaurants."

There were all kinds listed: Italian restaurants, Hungarian restaurants, seafood restaurants. One restaurant specialized in Greek cuisine; another boasted home cooking ("Mother's finest"). But

Bernie didn't see any that advertised German cooking. He looked and looked.

Finally, down in the corner of a page, he saw a small ad that said

RUDI'S
The Place for Authentic German Food
Located in Historic German Village.

This is what I'm looking for, Bernie thought, and he checked the address: 21 Green Street.

He closed the directory, hopped down off the chair, and went out the door of the employment office. The cat was gone.

He looked up and down the street. Where could German Village be? He sniffed the air. That didn't help. There was no smell of cooking anywhere, just the odor of automobile exhaust and rainy streets.

I'd better ask somebody, he thought, and he stopped an old man carrying a briefcase.

"Excuse me," said Bernie. "Could you direct me

to German Village? I'm new in town."

The old man cupped a hand to his ear and bent down. "Say again?"

Hard-of-hearing, thought Bernie, and he repeated his question.

"Berman Tillage?" The old man shook his head. "Never heard of him!"

Bernie asked a few more people. None of them could help him.

"Is that the old Indian village that was just dug up down by the river?" asked a man wearing a hard hat and carrying a lunch pail.

"I don't think so," answered Bernie. "That doesn't sound like it."

He was getting discouraged. And hungry. *Maybe the cat had the right idea,* he thought. *I'll lie down and take a nap.*

Later, when he awoke, the sun had gone behind some clouds and there was the faint sound of thunder. For a while, he just sat and looked around, yawned, and scratched his left ear.

Then, in front of him, he noticed a large sign that said in bold black letters PLACES TO GO. It listed an art museum, a science and engineering exhibit, an oriental display, *and* German Village. "German Village!" said Bernie. "There it is!"

HISTORIC GERMAN VILLAGE
Conveniently located five blocks
west—follow arrows

Encouraged, Bernie got up quickly and trotted to the curb. Right away he saw a large sign with an arrow and beneath the arrow, the words GERMAN VILLAGE STRAIGHT AHEAD.

He was on his way.

Chapter Four

∽∾∽

Down to Business

In the late afternoon, after a lot of walking, Bernie came to German Village. Right away he felt at home.

There were houses with wrought-iron fences and gardens filled with marigolds and roses. Brick streets were lined with lamps.

Bernie walked until he reached Green Street.

The restaurant was a small brick building with a faded black-and-white awning over the door. A sign said RUDI'S—AUTHENTIC GERMAN COOKING.

Bernie did not see many customers.

For a while, he just sat and looked at the restaurant. It seemed to be a friendly place. *But I wonder,* he thought, *will they chase me away?*

He decided not to hang around the front door, but went instead back to the alley, where hollyhocks grew thickly.

In the morning, he thought, *they'll find me on their doorstep.* With this in mind, he gave a deep sigh and curled up, nose to tail, to sleep.

Next day, Bernie awoke with a start to find Rudi and his wife, Ilse, looking down at him.

"Will you bite?" Ilse asked him, petting him cautiously. Bernie responded immediately by thumping his tail.

"Does he belong to anyone, do you think?" asked Rudi. "He doesn't have a collar." Bernie's little red collar was long gone.

"And he's so dirty!" Ilse exclaimed.

They looked him over. "Go on home now," said Rudi in a halfhearted manner. Bernie didn't move.

"Just a stray," said Ilse, shaking her head.

After a while, the two went inside.

Bernie stayed on the doorstep all day and all night. The next morning, close by, he found a bowl of water and some food, which he ate quickly. Food and water appeared every day after that. Occasionally, Ilse came out to look at him.

This may be the most I can ever expect, Bernie thought. However, one morning, he felt himself being lifted up and taken inside.

"Bath time," said Ilse.

Bernie was bathed and brushed till his brown-and-white coat felt like velvet. A new collar was waiting for him—a green one this time—and he was carried upstairs to the apartment above the restaurant, where there were three tiny rooms. In one of them, space had been found for a wicker dog bed, into which Bernie climbed gratefully.

Life was better now. He had fresh water and food regularly, and was looking forward to table scraps again.

One day Ilse scraped something into his dish.

"Pot roast, love," she said.

Bernie tasted it and pulled back. *Ugghhh! Terrible!* he thought.

"I don't think he's hungry, Ilse," said Rudi, looking concerned.

Ilse tried to tempt him with the best dishes from the restaurant menu—potatoes with sour cream dressing, sauerbraten, fish dumplings—but Bernie didn't eat much of it. He lost some weight.

"I'll make an appointment with the vet," said Rudi to Ilse one day. "He may be anemic and need some vitamins."

"No," said Bernie, coming forward quickly out of his dog bed. "It isn't that. It's . . . it's the food."

Rudi and Ilse stared in amazement at Bernie.

"Yes, the food," said Bernie. "I mean . . . it isn't right. The food isn't right."

"It isn't?" asked Ilse.

"No," said Bernie. "Take for instance the seasoning in that last batch of sauerbraten. It was all wrong. You could have used some grated lemon rind and a touch of bay leaf. And it should have been served with potato dumplings and hot stewed prunes."

Ilse and Rudi looked at Bernie.

"And the German rolled pancakes with jam. The pancakes were far too heavy, and apricot jam would have been good instead of strawberry. It would have been a change for the customers. By the way," Bernie added, "you seem to have very few customers."

Ilse nodded sadly. "Yes. The restaurant is failing. If business doesn't pick up, we're finished. We'll have to go back to Budapest."

"*Budapest*?" Bernie asked. "Do you mean Budapest, Hungary?"

"Yes," said Ilse.

"Then you're not even from Germany?"

"No," she admitted.

"Ahhh," said Bernie, "that explains it! You really don't know German cooking!"

"No," said Ilse, "but we use recipes given me by an aunt who was German . . . I think."

"I see," said Bernie. He thought for a moment. "I may be able to help you."

And for the next hour or so he talked about German food and his days at the Grubers.

"For a light luncheon salad," he said, "Mrs. Gruber sometimes made *Schinken mit Brunnenkresse*."

"*Schinken mit* what?" asked Ilse.

"Brunnenkresse," replied Bernie. "Watercress. Watercress and ham salad. Providing we can get a good supply of fresh, clean watercress, we'll mix a head of lettuce and some watercress in a salad bowl. Then in the center, pile diced ham mixed with chopped, cooked egg whites. And for the dressing . . . "

After a while, the three of them went downstairs to the kitchen.

"Did you ever try prune fritters?" asked Bernie, feeling right at home now. "You drain one pound of cooked prunes, about thirty-six—they should not be too soft—and then . . . "

With Bernie in charge of the kitchen, business really picked up. So much so, in fact, that customers had to be turned away.

"I hate to do that," Ilse complained.

"Maybe we could move somewhere else," suggested Rudi, "someplace bigger."

"No," said Ilse. "I like it here. The brick streets remind me of home."

"I have an idea," said Bernie. "There's a vacant lot next door. Perhaps you could buy it and expand."

Rudi nodded. "That might be possible."

"And you don't actually have to do any building," said Bernie. "You might just make an outdoor dining area. Then, at least in the good weather, you could seat more customers."

Ilse nodded. "That would be nice! We could have tables with umbrellas, and there could be flowers!"

"And while we're at it," said Bernie, "the kitchen and dining room need work. The stove is too small and the carpet is worn in the dining room."

So planning began.

The three worked through the fall.

Carpet was ripped up and replaced. In the front, a large window was added, and a big new stove and refrigerator were ordered. At the front door, in place of the old awning, a new black-and-white one with brass fittings was installed, and the outside trim of the building was painted a soft gray.

For the dining room, Rudi ordered a cuckoo clock straight from the Black Forest in Germany.

When Christmastime came, the restaurant was given a festive look with a small fir tree trimmed with bright ornaments and a fragrant wreath in the new window. And as a special treat for the children, Bernie made *schneeballen*—"snowballs"—of sweet cookie dough rolled, baked, and dusted with vanilla sugar.

Spring came, and work started on the outdoor area. The old lot was cleared and a flagstone patio was laid, with room in the center for a small flowering tree. To give privacy from the street, a fence was built.

"About the tables and umbrellas," Ilse asked Bernie one day. "What do you think?"

"Let's have the tables and chairs of white wrought iron," suggested Bernie, "and the umbrellas black and white to match our awning."

"Good idea," said Rudi.

The tables and chairs with their umbrellas were set out, along with pots of bright flowers, and blue morning glories were trained along the fence. All in all, on a nice day, it was a very pleasant place to sit and eat, and it soon became very popular.

One day Rudi said to Bernie, "Look out front." When Bernie looked, he saw that the sign had been changed. Now, instead of RUDI'S, it said BERNIE'S —AUTHENTIC GERMAN COOKING.

Ilse made Bernie a little white chef's hat with a strap under the chin, and a photographer took his picture for the local newspaper.

"You've become famous!" said Ilse, giving Bernie a hug.

Chapter Five

∿∿∿

Old Friends Meet Again

One warm Sunday afternoon that summer Bernie happened to glance outside. There, at one of the little tables, sat the Grubers. Mrs. Gruber was wearing a purple-flowered dress with a matching hat and having a piece of hazelnut cake with her coffee.

"My compliments to the chef," she said sweetly to Ilse.

Bernie walked out to the patio. The Grubers stared at him.

"That no-good dog!" said Mrs. Gruber quickly. "Or rather"—and she glanced around, smiling sheepishly —"*such* a good dog! I always said so, didn't I, Mr. Gruber?"

"Of course, dear," he answered. He was busy with his cake.

"*Such* an unusual dog! I always said that. Destined for great things in the kitchen."

"Thank you," said Bernie. "I had a good teacher."

Mrs. Gruber smiled broadly.

"I will say she had a heavy hand with the salt, however," said Bernie, "and a slight tendency to overcook, but all things considered, not a bad teacher."

"Well," said Mr. Gruber, wiping his mouth delicately with his napkin, "that wasn't bad cake!"

"I agree," said Mrs. Gruber in a huffy manner. "Of course, the icing was a bit stiff, and the nuts—were they old? They tasted somewhat stale. And," she added, "the cake *could* have been in the oven a little longer. My piece wasn't entirely done."

Autumn passed and November arrived, ending the outdoor dining. The umbrellas and tables were covered up, and everything was readied for the winter.

One night Bernie was working late in the kitchen. Outside, the wind had picked up and things were banging around in the alley. There was one loud noise in particular. *The garbage cans have blown over,* he thought.

He opened the door and looked out into the night. Snowflakes were glittering in the air. By the light of the kitchen, he saw a familiar shape run down the alley. Quickly he called to it.

"Red! Red! Come back! It's me, Bernie!"

Cautiously, a very dirty, bedraggled Red appeared. "Bernie? Is it really you?"

"Yes," answered Bernie, "it's me!" He looked around fearfully. "But where's Cutie? I hope nothing's happened to her!"

"Not exactly," said Red. "She did hurt her leg trying to get over a fence."

Slowly, out of the shadows, stepped Cutie, thinner than ever before and limping slightly.

Bernie opened the kitchen door. Light flooded out into the night. "Red, Cutie, come in here where it's warm!"

Slowly Bernie's two friends went into the kitchen. They hadn't been inside anywhere for a long, long time. "It took some getting used to," Red admitted later.

Quickly, Bernie served them both some leftover beef stew and a pan of water, and watched them gulp it down. "From now on," he promised, "you'll eat like this every day! You've found a home now!"

Over the next few weeks, Red and Cutie were bathed and brushed. Red's coat began to gleam again. And Ilse took Cutie to the grooming salon where she was trimmed up just like she used to be, with a little rhinestone bow by her left ear. And with a little rest and a warm place to sleep, her leg gradually healed.

Red helped out at the restaurant. His special job was keeping the cats away.

One night he came in the back door, shaking his head in exasperation.

"The cats around here! So many of them! One in particular, a big old tough cat with a torn ear, just keeps coming back!"

Bernie looked up from the stove where he was carefully preparing a custard filling to go into six huge cream puffs. "Big gray cat?" he asked. "With yellow eyes and a torn ear?"

"That's the one," answered Red.

Bernie thought for a minute. "I think I know that cat. . . . He's a friend of mine. Next time you see him, Red, don't chase him away. See if you can get him inside. And remind me," he added, "when I make out the grocery list tomorrow, to put plenty of tuna fish on it. And we'll see if we can't find a catnip ball, too. A blue one!"

From then on, the three friends stayed together,

living a busy, happy, comfortable life. The cat, whose
name turned out to be Tiger, joined them after quite
a bit of coaxing.

And Bernie, who was the happiest of all, became
very, very famous in the restaurant business.